Postman Pat and the Flood

Story by **John Cunliffe**

Pictures by **Ray Mutimer**

from the original Television designs by Ivor Wood

Hippo

Scholastic Children's Books,
Scholastic Publications Ltd,
7-9 Pratt Street, London NW1 0AE, UK

Scholastic Inc.,
555 Broadway, New York, NY 10012-3999, USA

Scholastic Canada Ltd,
123 Newkirk Road, Richmond Hill,
Ontario, Canada, L4C 3G5

Ashton Scholastic Pty Ltd
PO Box 579, Gosford, New South Wales,
Australia

Ashton Scholastic Ltd,
Private Bag 92801, Penrose, Auckland,
New Zealand

First published by Scholastic Publications Ltd. 1994
This edition published by Scholastic Publications Ltd, 1995

Text Copyright © John Cunliffe 1994
Illustrations copyright © Scholastic Publications Ltd and
Woodland Animations Ltd 1994
ISBN: 0 590 55793 9

Typeset in Infant Plantin by Rapid Reprographics
Printed in Belgium by Proost Book Production.

10 9 8 7 6 5 4 3 2 1

Katy and Tom were playing by the stream.
  "I'm going to make a dam," said Tom.
  "I'll help," said Katy.
  "Great!" said Tom. "Let's get our wellies on."

Their mum saw them. "That's sensible," she said. "Keep your feet dry."

They went out to the stream that runs in the field, just by
the yard.

"Look," said Tom, "there's a big stone. It'll be a good one to start with."

Tom couldn't lift it.

"Hang on," said Katy, "let me..."

They could lift it together, but only just. They dropped it into the middle of the stream. It splashed them all over!

"Never mind," said Tom, "we're wet now. We can't get much wetter."

They built a wall of stones across the stream. The water became deeper behind the wall, but it found little gaps where it could still get through.

"It's squeezing through," said Katy.

"Let's get some mud," said Tom, "that'll stop it."

Tom went for his spade. They dug up some squares of turf beside the wall.

"That'll be good," said Katy, "it's got clay in it. Clay can stop water."

It did. The water grew deeper behind their dam. Katy didn't notice how deep it was. She stepped into it to place another piece of turf.

"Ow! Oooooooh!" she cried.

The water had come over the top of her wellie. How cold it was!

"It's getting deep," said Tom.

Katy took her wellie off and poured the water out.

"It's a good dam," said Tom. "The best ever."

The ducks came to look. They didn't much like the dam, but they did like the pond that it had made. They went for a swim in it.

"Katy! Tom!"
That was mum calling them in to tea.
"Coming!" called Tom.

After tea it was bedtime. Katy and Tom didn't see how their pond was growing behind the dam. It grew bigger and bigger. The ducks had a great time dabbling and swimming in it.

During the night, it began to rain. There was more water coming down the stream. More water to fill the dam.

Katy and
Tom were asleep.

Mum and dad
were asleep.

The ducks were asleep.

None of them saw the pond behind the dam growing bigger and bigger. No one saw the water reaching across the yard.

No one saw it creeping under the kitchen door and making a new pond in the kitchen, getting deeper and deeper.

The water ran into the hen house. How the hens clucked
when they stepped in it!

The water ran into the barn. The cat was out hunting. She saw it.

She got her feet wet, and how she hated that! She shook her feet dry, and climbed high on a bale of straw.

What a good thing it was that Pat was so early with the post. He was the first person to see the flood. His van splashed through it in the yard.

He jumped out. "Never mind wet feet!" he said to Jess, but Jess stayed in the van. "Now where is it coming from?" said Pat.

He splashed through the water. He looked over the wall.
He saw Katy and Tom's dam.

"Oh, dear, they've been building a dam!"

He rolled up his trousers, and waded across the new pond.

Pat saw a big stone in the middle of the dam. He pulled it out. With a great whoooooooshhhhhh the water rushed through the gap.

The pond began to get smaller. Pat pulled more stones and mud out of the dam. Soon it was gone. The water ran away down the stream, and the new pond went with it.

"That's better," said Pat.

"That's *much* better," said Mrs Pottage, looking over the wall. "And thanks, Pat. Now you've got wet feet. Come in and have a hot drink, and I'll get you some dry socks, if anything *is* dry."

"And I'll get you some dry letters," said Pat.

Katy and Tom looked over the wall.
"Our dam!" said Tom.

"It was a good one," said Pat. "It nearly flooded Greendale. I was thinking of getting a boat instead of a van."

"It was *too* good," said Katy.
"*Much* too good," said Mrs Pottage firmly.